Goodnight kiss

Written by Jillian Harker

Illustrated by Andrew-Everitt-Stewart

p

KU-433-697

"It's bedtime now, Oakey," said Mum.

Oakey curled up in the chair.
His ears began to droop and he muttered,
"Oh, that's not fair!"

"Have a drink first," smiled Mum, "then you must go."
"Five minutes more!" begged Oakey.
Mum answered, "No!"

100 recipes for CARROTS

Oakey's ears drooped
and off he went.
But he was
back in a flash!

"What's the matter?"
asked Mum.

"There's a ghost
in the hallway, hovering around.
Look, there it is floating
just above the ground,"
he wailed.

"Oh, Oakey, you've made a mistake.
That's no ghost.
It's just an old coat, hanging on the hook.
Coats don't float!" laughed Mum.

Oakey's ears drooped and
off he went.
But he was
back in a flash!

"Why aren't you in bed, Oakey?"
asked Mum.

"There's a
great big lump
beneath the sheets.
It's waiting to get me.
I'm scared it's going to pounce.
Please come and see,"
sniffed Oakey.

"Oh, Oakey, you've made a mistake.
The only thing underneath the sheets,
is your old teddy bear," smiled Mum.

Oakey's ears drooped
and he got into bed.
But he didn't
close his eyes.

"Why aren't you asleep?"
asked Mum.

"There are
huge creepy crawlies
underneath my bed.
And I can't get the thought of them
out of my head,"
complained Oakey.

"They're just your slippers, Oakey, so there's no need to hide. They won't be creeping anywhere without your feet inside," grinned Mum. "That's it now, Oakey. Time to say goodnight."

Mum turned and left the room, switching off the light.

And then Oakey saw it,
standing by the door.
The monster!

It moved across the floor and
walked straight towards him,
with its arms stretched out.
Oakey's mouth opened,
but he found he couldn't shout.

The monster leaned over him
and Oakey closed his eyes. What
happened next gave Oakey an
enormous surprise. The monster
picked him up and cuddled him
tight. Monsters just don't do that.
This couldn't be right!

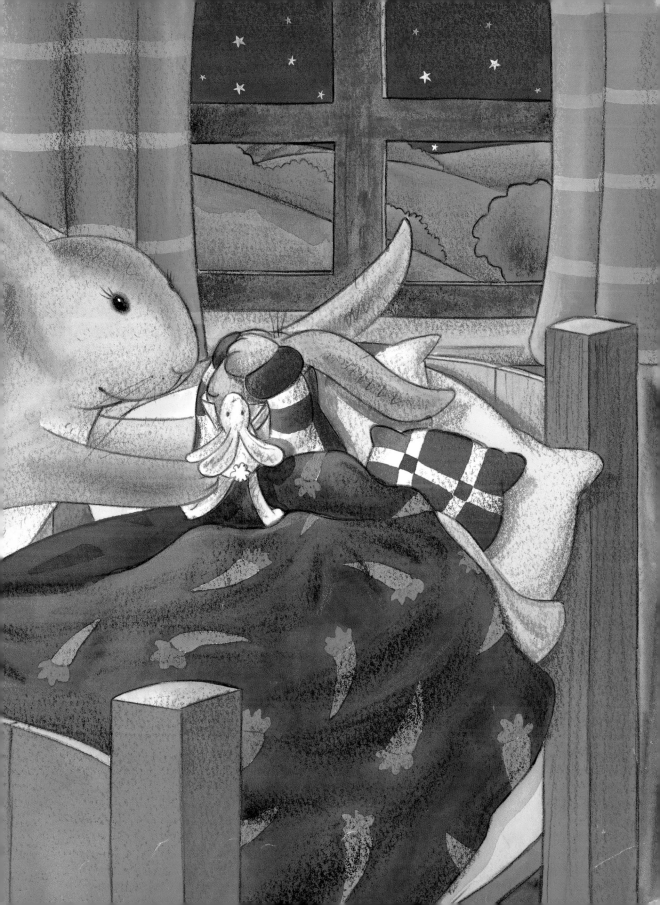

Then Mum's voice whispered,
"Don't worry, it's just me.
When I said 'Goodnight' just now,
I forgot to give you this."

Then 'Monster Mum' gave Oakey
a goodnight kiss!